Not a Creature Was Stirring?

Look for these SpineChillers™ Mysteries

#1   *Dr. Shivers' Carnival*
#2   *Attack of the Killer House*
#3   *The Venom Versus Me*
#4   *Pizza with Extra Creeps*
#5   *The Phantom of Phys Ed*
#6   *Not a Creature Was Stirring?*
#7   *Birthday Cake and I Scream*
#8   *Stay Away from the Swamp*
#9   *Tuck Me In, Mummy*
#10 *Stay Tuned for Terror*
#11 *Hospitals Make Me Sick*
#12 *A Haunted Mine Is a Terrible Thing to Waste*

Not a Creature Was Stirring?

Fred E. Katz

Thomas Nelson, Inc.

Nashville

Published in Nashville, Tennessee, by Tommy Nelson™, a division of Thomas Nelson, Inc. SpineChillers™ Mysteries is a trademark of Thomas Nelson, Inc.

Scripture quoted from the *International Children's Bible, New Century Version,* copyright © 1986, 1988 by Word Publishing. Used by permission.

Storyline: Tim Ayers

ISBN 0-8499-4061-3

Printed in the United States of America

97 98 99 00 01 02 QKP 9 8 7 6 5 4 3 2 1

"I can't believe it. I just can't believe it! How could this happen? Why now?" I yelled the whole way back from the hospital. I wasn't usually such a crybaby, and my parents didn't let me get away with self-pity often. But this was a big disappointment for me.

My folks had been invited to speak at a marriage-counseling conference. It was to be held in the mountains the week before Christmas. They had planned to stay on and take me skiing afterward. *Why did I have to break my leg?*

Months ago, Dad had promised to take me on this trip. I love to ski. I love having the cold air blowing past my face as I hurtle down the slopes.

Now because of the broken leg, I couldn't go.

If only I hadn't worked out on the last day of school before Christmas vacation. My buddy Glen and I had spent some time challenging each other. He showed off his best gymnastics move, and I had to try to copy it. Then I made my moves, and he had to try mine.

The difference is, Glen is a little better and a little more daring than I am.

He did his special routine on the rings. I tried to imitate him and completely blew it.

So I climbed onto the parallel bars—my best event—for my challenge. I started by swinging my midsection over the bar and circling it for my mount. I was hot-dogging, and I knew it. If I wanted to win the challenge, I had to do something he couldn't do.

I did a handstand on the bars, then I dropped into a somersault between them. I looked pretty good.

The dismount was next. I swung myself up, let go of the bars, and did a somersault in midair.

I felt so good, I forgot to keep my focus. I started thinking about how wide with awe Glen's eyes probably were.

My distraction was my downfall. Literally.

I was too close to the floor as I came out of my head-over-heels dismount.

C-r-a-c-k . . .

The pain only took moments to hit my brain. I knew immediately that I had broken my leg. *The ski trip!*

When Dad and Mom got to the hospital, I grabbed Dad's arm and begged, "Please don't leave me here!"

Dad looked touched. He squeezed my shoulder. "Don't worry, Conner, we're not leaving you. The doctor said you can go home today."

"No!" I said, realizing he misunderstood. "I'm not afraid of the hospital. I mean, please don't leave me at home. Can I still go on the ski trip?"

"Son, I know you were looking forward to this trip," Mom said, "but even if you came along, you couldn't ski. I'm sure you wouldn't enjoy watching TV in a hotel room all day. And we wouldn't be comfortable leaving you by yourself in a town we don't know. Aunt Bergen has already agreed to come to watch the house. She can keep an eye on you too."

"You just concentrate on healing that leg," Dad added. "There will be other ski trips."

"Now, how about our getting you home?" Mom said.

When we got to the house, Mom helped me get settled in the living room. The Christmas tree and other decorations surrounded me.

I looked at the tabletop nativity scene. It had been in my mom's family since she was a little girl. Every year we carefully placed the porcelain figurines on the table and talked about the true meaning of Christmas.

I've always felt happy at Christmas. Until now. I was having a really hard time not wallowing in self-pity. Then I had a thought.

Mom was in the kitchen getting out plates for the pizza we had ordered when we got home. I called out, "Mom, since I've got to stay home, I can watch the house. Your aunt doesn't have to come, right?"

She dried her hands on a dish towel as she walked into the living room. "Wrong. I couldn't leave you home alone. The only reason I'm comfortable leaving you is that I know Aunt Bergen will be here with you."

"Mom, I've never even met her. I don't really want to have a stranger around while I'm trying to heal my broken leg."

Mom gave me a big smile. But I could tell my appeal hadn't worked.

She perched on the arm of my easy chair and leaned against the back.

4

"This is tough for you, isn't it?" she asked, brushing a strand of hair away from my eyes. "I can remember missing a horse show when I was ten because I broke my arm. Not fun. But the Great Physician took care of me then, and he'll take care of you now. You won't be lonely with him at your side.

"Besides, I'll bet Aunt Bergen will love having a little family around during the holiday. She's out of this world. I'm sure you'll have the time of your life. She used to take care of my brother and me when we were kids. We had such a crazy time; we never knew for sure what she was up to. She used to just about kill us."

Mom got up to head back into the kitchen. Over her shoulder, she continued, "I've never known anyone else quite like her. She and Uncle Charlie have traveled all over the world."

The doorbell rang. I managed to hobble to the front door with my crutches fairly quickly. I even beat Mom, but maybe she hadn't heard the bell.

I turned the doorknob and opened the door. I had expected to see the pizza delivery guy's face smiling at me from behind a box of pizza.

Instead, I saw a flash of red and white. Something smashed into me and nearly sent me flying backward.

Santa Claus? A red suit and red hat had pushed through the doorway. An inflatable Santa had me pinned against the door.

From behind Santa, Dad's big hand reached out to grab me.

"Hold it, Conner. I don't want you to fall and break another bone," he said.

I sighed with relief, but before I could straighten up I saw someone peering at me from a black hood. Her eyes sparkled at me. She wiggled past my father and grabbed me in a bear hug.

"So this is Conner. Young man, you look just like your grandfather did at this age. The spitting image!" She flipped her hood off, and I could see she wore her straight gray hair pulled back in a bun. She had it pinned in place with a fascinating comb. It was decorated with tiny faces that changed their expressions when she moved.

How do they do that? I wondered as I heard my

mother enter the room and exclaim, "Aunt Bergen! You're here!"

Aunt Bergen's arms shot out and quickly embraced Mom in a firm hug.

"Oh, my. You're all grown up. I always knew my favorite grand-niece would turn out well. And your son, Conner, is absolutely delightful," Aunt Bergen said. Her words flowed rapidly. "Now, how can I help?"

"Just knowing that you'll be here with Conner is enough," Mom said with a big smile. "Let me help you get settled in the spare bedroom upstairs."

They chattered happily as they climbed the stairs together. I hobbled back into the living room to keep out of everyone's way.

The evening was filled with laughter as the grown-ups caught up and packed. I wasn't in the mood to share in their joy. Sure, I'd studied Colossians 1:24 and knew to be "happy in my sufferings." But I wasn't doing a very good job of it. I guess it was a little rude, but I think everybody understood when I went to bed without saying goodnight.

By the time I crawled out of bed the next morning, Mom and Dad's luggage stood waiting in the entry hall. In a few minutes we would be saying good-bye. I had always thought it would be fun to have the house to myself. But suddenly I felt very alone. Even though we were related, I barely knew the woman I'd be staying with. I knew my parents would be back before Christmas Eve, but this was already feeling like the loneliest Christmas ever.

When the airport van arrived a few minutes later, Aunt Bergen hugged my parents good-bye. Then she disappeared into the kitchen while Dad carried the bags out to the curb.

Mom hung back to hug me. She whispered, "Aunt Bergen is even crazier than I remembered. There's something you need to know about her. She's—"

Dad came back inside to get Mom and interrupted her. "We'd better hurry if we're going to get to our plane in time."

"What do I need to know, Mom?" I asked, but Mom was already grabbing her gloves and running toward the door. I guess she didn't hear me ask.

As she stepped onto the porch, Mom turned back to me. She had a serious look on her face as she said quietly, "Watch out! Not everything is as it seems. Aunt Bergen is not quite like everyone else."

By the time I hobbled to the doorway, Mom had already gotten into the van.

What did she mean when she said that Aunt Bergen was not quite like everyone else? And last night she'd said that Aunt Bergen was out of this world. Was Aunt Bergen some sort of alien?

The van pulled out of the driveway and drove off toward the airport. I turned slowly on my crutches to make my way into my parents' bedroom. Because my room was upstairs—a really long climb on crutches—I was going to spend the next few days down here in their room.

I came face to face with Aunt Bergen.

"I've got a nice glass of milk for you. A growing boy with a broken bone needs one of these several times a day," she said as she smiled at me. All I could do was smile back. She carried the glass into the bedroom, and I followed her.

"Isn't this a wonderful time of the year?" Aunt Bergen's voice danced with happiness.

"I suppose for some kids it might be," I responded like Scrooge.

"Do I hear a bit of 'Bah, humbug' in your voice? What would a kid not like about Christmas?" she asked.

"Don't get me wrong, Aunt Bergen, I like presents as much as the next guy, but that seems to be all people think about these days."

"You think so?" Aunt Bergen's eyes were twinkling, but I could tell she was taking me seriously. "Go on."

"Every year I see my mom work hard trying to make Christmas special for Dad and me. If she isn't at the malls shopping, she's in the kitchen cooking. I wish it were different. I wish . . ."

"Yes?" she prompted.

"I wish we could take the food and presents to

somebody who maybe can't afford to buy any," I said. My words sort of surprised me. I didn't know Aunt Bergen, but I was telling her what was in my heart.

"Ah," Aunt Bergen said after a moment. "So Conner turned out just like his mom. Sounds like you appreciate all your mother does for you, and it sounds like she still puts others before herself.

"Do you know what your mother used to do when she was a girl? She always saved some of her Christmas toys for a special friend at church. The little girl's father had been killed in a car wreck. Your mom said she didn't like having so much when her friend had so little."

After a moment's thought, Aunt Bergen said with a smile, "I don't think your mother has changed much. Here it is the week before Christmas, and she and your dad are heading to a marriage conference to help others. I'm sure they'd really like to be here with you. I guess Christmas gifts come in all shapes and sizes. Maybe the best ones are the gifts you give of yourself."

She mussed up my hair. "Go ahead and drink your milk, honey. I have a feeling you're going to like this Christmas after all—broken leg or no broken leg."

She disappeared down the hall, leaving me alone with the milk and my thoughts.

I drank my milk and snuggled into the pillows for

11

a quick nap. Had my mother really given her brand-new Christmas toys away when she was my age? And was I being too hard on my parents for leaving me alone with Aunt Bergen? Lots of questions ran through my mind as I drifted off to sleep.

I was deep in sleep when I heard a faint tapping at my door. Groggily I limped to the door and opened it. My eyes flew open and I stumbled back—wide awake.

What a ghastly green face!

"Oh my!" said the green face as a hand reached out toward me. "Did I scare you? I forgot how strange this green mud pack on my face can look. I just thought you might like another glass of milk."

I choked out a thank you as she closed the door.

As my heart started to calm down, I stared at the glass she had handed me. After taking a sip, I set the milk on the nightstand. Then I picked up my book, which I had brought down from my room earlier. The book flipped open at the bookmark. It was a great story about four kids visiting California who get caught up in a really bizarre carnival. I didn't want to stop reading, but a noise distracted me.

It sounded like some sort of moaning. Was something hurt? I had to find out where the noise was coming from.

I moved slowly and quietly. I opened the door and peeked into the hallway. I didn't see anything unusual, but I briefly heard the moaning again. I crutched quietly down the hall toward the kitchen.

When I got to the kitchen, I heard another moan. Where was Aunt Bergen? The sound was louder than before. I was getting closer.

I took another step, then stopped. The moaning had stopped. I moved again, and the sound began again.

The noise had to be coming from the basement. The stairs down were just across the kitchen from me. I hobbled toward the basement door.

Fear kept me from opening it and going down to explore. I knew I had to do so if I wanted to find out what the sound was.

What's in our basement? What if Aunt Bergen is an alien and she's captured someone?

I stood there a moment, trying to decide what to do.

Jesus, I finally prayed, *you're going to have to go with me. I'm too scared to check this out by myself.*

My hand stretched toward the doorknob. I hesitated. My heart was pounding inside my chest.

I had to do it right away before I chickened out. I grabbed the doorknob.

A loud pounding rang through the house.

What was going on?

Was something trying to get out?

Or was something trying to get in?

14

Almost relieved to be distracted from the basement stairs, I stumbled into the hallway.

Whatever was doing the pounding sounded strong enough to do some damage to me if I wasn't careful.

I crept closer. The banging seemed so loud. It had to be coming from the hall closet.

Without hesitating to give myself time to be afraid, I yanked the closet door open. Something big and red jumped at me. I took an uncoordinated step backward and grabbed the stair railing for balance. It stopped me from smashing to the floor. I slid down the wall as the red form floated slowly toward me.

"The inflatable Santa Claus again! This is the second time it's attacked me, and the second time it's won," I grumbled.

The pounding startled me again. I realized it was coming from the front door.

Feeling sort of foolish for letting my imagination

get away from me, I grabbed my crutches. As I worked my way to the front door, I put together an apology for taking so long to answer. I eased the front door open. A large brown box was thrust into my face. It seemed to be suspended in the air.

A voice from inside the box asked, "Are you Conner Morgan?"

I was stunned. A flying box had asked me a question. I answered, "What?"

The box spoke again. "Are you Conner Morgan?"

"Yes, I am. But what are you? How do you do that? Who sent you?" I asked in rapid-fire succession.

"Do you want it under the tree, kid?" the box questioned, sounding a little tired.

"You can do that?" I wondered aloud. This was the greatest thing I had ever seen. Was it done by remote? Who controlled it?

The box pushed its way past me as I stumbled backward to get out of its way. It took me a second to regain my balance and close the door. By that time the box had floated into the living room and out of sight. *A flying box,* I thought, *is something I should keep my eye on.*

I hobbled into the living room. The white lights on the Christmas tree lit up the dried flowers and ornaments scattered all through it. Suddenly I realized I was looking at an elf.

His green hat and green suit almost blended in

with the tree. He jumped over the gifts and bounded toward me. I stopped, stunned.

"There it is, kid. I just need your signature right here," the elf said as I stared in amazement.

"Could you please tell me what's going on?" I asked him. I guess the sounds from the basement and the surprise attack from the inflatable Santa had rattled me. I certainly hadn't been expecting a present—or an elf.

"I work for Elf Express. This time of year our delivery service is hopping," he explained. "Merry Christmas, kid."

He left as quickly as he had come. I heard him shut the front door behind him.

Curious about where the present came from, I was just about to examine the package. But someone started pounding on the front door again. I thought maybe the delivery elf had forgotten something.

I guided my crutches to the front door and yanked it open with a big smile on my face. Only I didn't find the elf.

A single thought ran through my mind: *How did this snowman get here?*

"Argh!"

I slammed the door. Too many weird things were happening. I couldn't take it all in.

I heard the pounding again, louder than ever. Then the doorbell rang repeatedly. I peeked out the window beside the door. A pair of human eyes peered out from under a snow-covered stocking cap. I recognized one of the kids from our church. He was covered with snow.

I felt a little embarrassed when I slowly opened the door again. "Sorry. I thought you were a snowman."

"A snowman?"

"Yeah. It's been a crazy morning. Sorry I slammed the door in your face."

"That's okay," he said. "Everyone from the youth group is sledding down the churchyard hill. I was going to ask you to join us, but it looks like you can't go. Sorry you hurt yourself."

"Thanks." He was a nice guy. I'd have liked to go

sledding with him. After I told him the story of how I broke my leg, we agreed to try again when my leg healed. He wished me a Merry Christmas as he ran back toward the church.

Disappointed, I shut the door. Then I remembered the package. I hopped to the living room and looked under the tree. The box had my name on it.

I dragged it a little way from the tree so I could maneuver my cast around to sit beside it. I pulled the tape off the flaps. They popped open. Inside, I saw a smaller box. It was wrapped in red and green paper that said MERRY CHRISTMAS all over it.

Someone had taped a card to the top. Curious, I peeled the envelope open, pulled the card out of it, and read, "MERRY CHRISTMAS FROM YOU KNOW WHO."

But I didn't know who. I lifted the gift out of the box and shook it. It didn't rattle. *Maybe there's nothing in the box,* I thought. There was only one way to find out. Even though it wasn't Christmas yet, I'd felt so disappointed about this season that I barely even felt guilty about opening the gift early. I started ripping at the wrapping, sending paper flying everywhere.

Once I got all the Christmas wrap off, I still couldn't tell what was inside. I held a white box, and that box was taped together by somebody with lots of tape and lots of time.

What could I use to cut the tape? I looked around the room. Mom's letter opener was sitting on the end table next to me. What a break! I didn't even need to move. I reached for the opener and started breaking through the tape. The box top popped open.

Inside was a brightly colored metal box. It looked like the sort of tin that Christmas cookies come in. Why had someone sent me cookies and not signed the gift?

I grabbed the top of the tin and twisted it off.

The moment it loosened, the lid flew into the air. Something sprang from the box and landed in my lap.

A snake!

I pushed it off my lap and tried to scramble to my feet—no easy task with a cast and crutches.

My hardware forced me to slow down. When I did, I took a closer look at the "snake." I realized it was actually a weird-looking fantasy creature. It looked like something from another galaxy. I saw that it had a spring attached so it could jump; that's how it flew out of the box. Taped to the creature's body was a note. I bent over and detached the piece of paper to read it.

> *Dear Conner,*
> *We wanted to send you a little something to let you know we miss you already. Aunt Bergen is something else, isn't she?*
>
>

Love,
Mom and Dad

Whew! I was glad Mom and Dad missed me as much as I missed them, but my heart was still pounding a bit from the creature's leap. After all this excitement, I decided I needed a drink of water. As I headed toward the kitchen, I heard a quiet moan. I had completely forgotten about the sounds in the basement.

I walked as softly as I could down the hallway. Suddenly I heard more than moaning in the basement. Something fell over and landed with a bang.

What was that? I hobbled faster toward the door to the basement steps. Again I wondered where Aunt Bergen had disappeared to. I decided I really needed to investigate downstairs and reached for the doorknob.

But before I could pull the door open, it slammed into me. I staggered back and barely kept from falling over.

As I struggled to remain upright, I heard a little yelp.

I looked up and saw Aunt Bergen. She looked startled; her eyes were wide with surprise.

"Oh, my. I'm so sorry, Conner. I didn't know you were in the kitchen. I hope I didn't scare you as much as you scared me," she said with one of her big, friendly smiles.

"I heard some odd sounds coming from the basement, and I wondered what was making them. I was just about to investigate. What's going on?" I asked.

"Nothing for you to worry your little head about," she insisted. "Let's get you back to your parents' room. Maybe you can watch a video or something."

She seemed awfully insistent that I leave the kitchen. I wondered why.

As she ushered me back toward Mom and Dad's room, she said, "I thought I heard pounding up here. What was it? Did someone come to the door?"

"It was a delivery person. I got a gift from my parents," I answered.

"How wonderful! I know they're always thinking of you. I hope it was something cheerful. Well, here we are—let's get you settled in bed again. Which video do you want to watch?" she asked.

"Aunt Bergen, I don't want to watch a video. I want to know what's going on in the basement," I said.

"I don't think it's a good idea for you to climb down those stairs with that cast on. I've been down there. There's nothing for you to worry about." She smiled even bigger.

I wasn't sure I believed her, but I knew she wasn't going to let me go down there. Something—or some-one—was in our basement. Something that made the oddest sounds. Even if I couldn't see it now, I knew that at some point she would be out of the house, and I'd sneak down there.

As Aunt Bergen helped me get comfortable, I thought about everything that had happened since I broke my leg. I decided I had to stay alert and keep my eyes wide open. I was afraid of what would hap-pen to me. Maybe a little prayer time would calm my nerves. I used the remote to turn off the video Aunt Bergen had started for me.

Aunt Bergen had gone into the living room to lis-ten to Christmas music. I could hear it too. I couldn't let myself fall asleep. But in spite of my resolve, my eyes dropped shut. When I forced them back open, I noticed something in the room that I hadn't seen before. Above the bed on the wall was a wreath made of holly. I wondered who had put it there.

To stay awake, I sat up and reached for my Bible. It wasn't where I'd left it. I must have knocked it off the nightstand somehow. I began to swing my legs out of the bed when something snagged me from behind.

Startled, I struggled to catch my breath. What had grabbed me? Had Aunt Bergen tiptoed into the room? Had the mysterious presence gotten loose from the basement?

Something started to snake its way around my neck. I reached up and felt sharp leaves and little hard berries. Holly? I looked up at the wreath above the bed. It had sprouted strange little vining branches that crept along the headboard. Two strong vines had reached around my body.

Struggling to free myself, I pulled at the branch at my neck. As I got free, the vine curled around my waist.

I realized I had to come up with a strategy. And I had to do it quickly. More holly was working its way back to my neck.

The thought hit me: *When Mom cuts holly in the backyard, she uses strong scissors. Where can I get a pair of scissors?*

Then I remembered that Mom kept a small pair in her nightstand drawer. As I grappled with the holly, I inched myself closer to the nightstand. I shot my

hand out and pulled the drawer open. The scissors
were there! I reached for them. My fingers touched
the cold metal. I had them! I hoped they were strong
enough.

I began slashing at the holly. It fell away from my neck and arms. My body was loose, but as I struggled to get away, something grabbed my ankle!

A spooky voice called my name, "Conner, Conner." The voice sounded fuzzy.

Again it said, "Conner, Conner. Wake up. You're having a nightmare." I suddenly recognized Aunt Bergen's voice. I must have fallen asleep. I'd been having a nightmare! My imagination had definitely worked overtime.

"Thanks, Aunt Bergen. I was having a pretty scary dream. I thought I was being choked by a holly wreath. What's crazy is that there isn't even a holly wreath in this room. See?" I said as I pointed upward.

I stopped abruptly. "Where did that come from?"

Aunt Bergen gave me a big smile. "I found it in the garage and thought it would cheer up this room. I had hoped that it would help you get into the Christmas spirit," she said.

"Could you take it away?" I asked. "After my dream, that wreath gives me a funny feeling."

She reached up and pulled the wreath from the wall. Then she quietly slipped out of the room.

How strange, I thought. *First Aunt Bergen arrives, and I hear strange sounds from the basement. Then Aunt Bergen puts a wreath up, and I have one of the worst nightmares of my life. What's going on?*

To distract myself for a while, I turned on the TV. An old version of *A Christmas Carol* by Charles Dickens was playing. It was one of my favorite Christmas specials.

When I was little, I used to get really scared whenever Scrooge's partner, Marley, came to visit him. Just the sound of his chains rattling and clanking was enough to make me hide behind the couch.

As I watched, Marley left Scrooge. Suddenly chains started clanking somewhere in the house.

I should have known that if ever there was a day that chains would clank down the hallways of my house, it would be today. My ears sometimes deceive me, but this time they were finely tuned to the sounds.

The clattering chain links rumbled, clanked, and bounced. I couldn't tell which was thumping louder, my heart or the chains.

My first reaction was to slip down under the covers. Then I realized that was a pretty lame idea. A thin flower-printed sheet, a fleece blanket, and a quilt wouldn't keep out a ghost that could pass through doors.

There was no place to go. The chains clanked and scraped along the wood hallway floor. I could tell that they were just outside the door to my parents' bedroom. I was about to find out what lurked on the other side.

Thump, thump, thump. Something pounded at the door. It shook with each blow. The knob turned, and the door slowly swung open.

I yelled, "I'm ready for you!"

But I wasn't.

I closed my eyes tight and pulled the covers over my head. The clanking came straight toward me.

It stopped just inches away. I could hear someone breathing, but I was too scared to look.

I felt a hand touch me.

"Ahh! Get away from me," I yelled as I scooted across the bed.

A now-familiar voice said, "Goodness. Did I do it again? I was only bringing you a little snack."

It was Aunt Bergen. I yanked the covers from my head. There she stood, holding a plate full of cookies and a glass of milk. The chains from our old porch swing were thrown over her shoulders, dangling to the floor. She noticed that I was staring at them.

"I found these in the basement. They will work perfectly," she gleefully told me.

"Work perfectly for what?" I asked.

"That, my dear nephew, is a surprise," she whispered. Aunt Bergen set the snack down on the nightstand, grabbed the empty glasses, and scurried out the door.

I heard her go back to the kitchen and then out to the garage.

Something was going on, and I wanted to know what. I decided that the first chance I got, I was going to explore the basement.

I sipped my milk and munched a cookie as I settled back on the pillows to watch the end of the movie. The Ghost of Christmas Present had just left Scrooge when a big clock gonged.

It gonged again.

Then the grandfather clock in our living room struck. I jumped. I'd broken that clock years ago. I couldn't believe I was hearing it now.

Dragging myself out of bed, I hobbled toward the door. I had to find out how the broken clock had chimed. When I reached the door, I stopped.

Aunt Bergen was clearly talking to someone.

Who could it be? I hadn't heard anyone come in. Could it be the mysterious moaner from the basement?

I silently opened the door just enough so that I could see into the living room. The voices were coming from there. I recognized Aunt Bergen's voice, but the other one sounded weird. At first I thought it might be a kid. Then it sounded more like a cartoon character. I couldn't see who was talking.

I opened the door an inch wider, and I saw a small hand resting on the back of a chair. It stood right across from my doorway.

I closed my eyes and opened the door wider as my fear grew.

When I opened my eyes, I was looking straight into the wooden face of a dummy. His left eyelid closed then opened again.

He had winked at me!

I stared. The dummy was dressed in a blue jacket with matching pants. A red bow tie and white sneakers completed the outfit. His wooden head was topped by a bunch of spiky red hair.

Where had he come from? I had never seen him before. Had he been hiding in our basement? Was he the mysterious noise maker?

I heard Aunt Bergen say, "Boris, are you enjoying your stay with my nephew?"

"Sure. He's the first kid I've ever met who has two wooden legs like me," Boris answered.

"Those are crutches," she said.

"Whatever you need to get you through," he remarked. "Hey, Bergen the Bedazzling, when am I going to do my little specialty for the boy?"

"Not until everyone is together," she answered. Then she giggled. "You're such a cutup; you'll kill them."

I gulped. What did she mean? He was a *cutup?* Who would he *kill?*

Again, I wondered about Aunt Bergen. She didn't act like anybody else I knew.

I quietly closed the door and leaned against the wall. I don't know how long I stood there lost in thought.

Suddenly the door flew open.

"Ah—Aunt Bergen! What are you doing there?" I gasped.

Aunt Bergen was standing, startled, in the doorway. "Oh my. What are you doing out of bed? I just came to see if you needed anything. Perhaps another glass of milk?" she asked with a big smile.

"You just brought me a glass," I told her.

"Hmmm. You're absolutely right. Do you know what the first two things to go when you get older are, Conner?" she asked with a hint of a smile.

"No, I don't," I said to humor her.

"The first is your memory and the second is . . . I forget what the second is." Aunt Bergen told her joke and gave me a big laugh.

I nodded with a slight smile. But I was thinking about something else. I wanted to get into the living room to see Boris up close.

"I think I'd like to sit in the living room awhile," I said as I tried to peek over her shoulder.

"I think it would be best if you stayed in bed. We don't want to put too much pressure on your healing leg. Perhaps you shouldn't walk on it," she said.

I knew she was just trying to keep me out of the living room. But I had an idea.

"I've been thinking, Aunt Bergen," I began. "Maybe you're right. I need to try harder to get into the Christmas spirit. If I spend some time in the living room with the tree, the ornaments, and the dum—, I mean, the gifts, I'll bet I can feel more festive," I said.

She bought my excuse with an encouraging smile and moved out of the way.

As I entered the living room, a quick look around told me that Boris was no longer on the chair. Where had he gone?

I furtively searched every possible place he might be hiding. I didn't want Aunt Bergen to notice that I was looking for Boris. I was so intent on my mission that the sudden hand on my shoulder made me jump.

"Ahh!" I yelped.

"Golly. It looks like I've done it again," she said remorsefully. "You certainly are jumpy. I thought I was the only one who started so easily. I've always thought it's because there aren't many around where I live," she confessed.

"Many *what* around?" I asked.

"People," she answered.

"What is around where you live?"

"You know, little things. Some are quite ancient. Some are quite unusual." Aunt Bergen looked a little sad. Then she changed the subject. "Well, I need to get some chores done." She turned and left. I guessed Aunt Bergen didn't want to answer any more questions.

I turned to start searching for Boris again. When I turned toward the Christmas tree, I noticed some new ornaments on it. I'd never seen anything like them.

They were deep red, deep blue, and deep green. They looked like glass or crystal. Curious, I got closer to them. I noticed that some held Christmas scenes from what looked like old English villages.

Some of the ornaments had faces in them. They looked three-dimensional. One in particular caught my attention. The face inside the glass ball was my mother's! I reached out to touch it. The ball moved slightly, and the face inside it gave me a smile. I snatched my hand back. Did I really see that?

These ornaments had to have come from Aunt Bergen. How had she shrunk my mother's head into a glass ball? What was she planning to do to me? Would she shrink my head, too? Then I remembered the odd comb she had been wearing when she first arrived. It had the faces that moved on it. Whose were they? Was each face a trophy of some sort?

As these frightening thoughts flew through my mind, I heard a horrible crash out in the garage. I decided I should investigate. But before I could get near the door leading to the garage, Aunt Bergen's familiar voice said, "Don't worry about the noise, Conner. I've already gone to check it out. A box fell off a shelf, but nothing broke. Why don't you go back to your parents' room and get some more rest?" she suggested. "That's the best thing you can do for your leg."

I wasn't going to be distracted that easily. Was I supposed to believe that story about a box falling?

Anyway, a box of what? It had sounded heavy, like a box full of horseshoes or something—not like anything we kept in the garage.

I needed to get help, but I didn't want to tip Aunt Bergen off. I obediently went into my folks' room.

There I picked up the phone and called my friend Glen. He lived right across the street. "Can you come over for a while? My Aunt Bergen, who has come to stay with me while Mom and Dad are gone, is really weird. I think she's some kind of alien," I said.

Glen started to say he'd be right over, then he hesitated. Finally he said, "I really want to, but my mom wants me to watch my little sister while she does some Christmas shopping. If I come over, Carrie will have to come too. Is that okay?"

"The more, the better. Aunt Bergen can't get us all. See you in a few minutes," I told him. I hung up the phone and started toward the front door. I figured it might take me as long to get there as it would take Glen and Carrie to cross the street.

In the hallway, I almost bumped into Aunt Bergen. I told her that a couple of kids were coming over to keep me company.

"What a lovely idea. Children seem so very sweet these days. I could just eat you all up," she said.

I'll bet that's exactly what you'd like to do, I thought, unhappy at the idea. Of course, I'd never say such a

43

thing out loud. Instead I said, "They should be here any minute."

The doorbell rang.

Glen has always been my number-one best friend. He is my exact age—we were born on the same day, only hours apart. The only difference was that I was born on the East Coast and he was born out West. We've been in the same class and attended the same church since kindergarten.

I pulled the door open and was happy to see his freckled face.

His sister, Carrie, was with him. She's two years younger than we are and isn't afraid of anything. In fact, her favorite thing to do is solve mysteries. I was glad she had come to help.

I introduced my friends to Aunt Bergen, who practically beamed at them.

Then she said, "As long as your friends are here to keep you company, I'd like to go out and run a few errands. Is that okay with you, Conner?"

When I nodded yes, she excused herself to get her cape from her room upstairs.

"She seems pretty nice," Glen said. "What's so weird about her?"

"Shh. She's right above us. I'll bet she's listening to everything we're saying, and you may be the next one she takes care of," I warned.

"What's happening around here? You sound totally scared," Carrie whispered.

44

I hobbled toward the bedroom door and said to Glen and Carrie, "Follow me. As soon as she's gone, I'll—"

"As soon as I'm gone, you'll do what?"

Aunt Bergen was standing in the bedroom doorway.

13

"Aunt Bergen!" I exclaimed.

"What do you have planned for when I'm gone?" she asked again.

I thought quickly. "I want to wrap your gift, and I don't want you to see it," I said. That was true. I did have a gift for her that I needed to wrap. Of course, I wasn't sure if I'd get to it right away because I had some investigating to do first.

Aunt Bergen smiled at us all as she put on her cape. "I don't think I'll be gone long. Bye, kids. Be good," she told us.

The moment the door shut, I led Glen and Carrie toward the garage. I wanted to see what had really fallen out there. As we walked through the house, I told them about my almost-encounter with Boris and how he had disappeared.

"I heard a story once about somebody getting stuffed into a chimney," Carrie said. "Let's look there. Maybe we'll find Boris."

Glen and I followed her back to the living room.

Carrie hesitated and then stuck her head into the fireplace to look up the chimney.

She immediately pulled back, ran to the couch, and buried her face in a pillow.

Glen and I were puzzled. "What?"

"Someone *is* up there. I saw the bottoms of two shoes."

Glen walked quickly across the room to the fireplace, bent over, and cautiously looked up. He quickly spun around and sat down hard on the floor. He looked as if he had seen a ghost.

"Is there really someone up there, Glen?" I pressed.

"Yes, just like Carrie said. You can see the bottoms of some shoes." Glen looked at me kind of funny.

"What do we do now?" I asked in astonishment.

"Maybe we can get him out of there," Glen suggested.

"I think we should try," Carrie answered.

Glen scratched his chin and then rubbed his temples. Then he said, "I guess the only thing we can do is grab his legs and try to pull him out."

It was a simple plan. Glen and Carrie stuck their heads back into the fireplace. With their hands, they each grabbed a foot and pulled. Instantly, the stuck mystery person fell toward them. One shoe

48

whacked Carrie on the nose. The other one kicked Glen's lower lip. Neither one seemed to be hurt.

When I saw the feet, I started to laugh. "Santa Claus was in the chimney!" I pointed as I spoke.

Glen and Carrie twisted themselves around to see that they had pulled on black boots with red pants tucked into them.

"It's that silly decoration that's been floating around here. I guess Aunt Bergen got tired of it jumping out of the closet at her," I confessed.

"Hmmm," Glen said. "Maybe all we'll find in the garage are more Christmas decorations."

"Let's go find out," Carrie said as she led the two of us to the garage door.

I took a deep breath. I was pretty sure we'd find more than decorations out there.

We opened the garage door. It was very dark inside.

The light switch was one step to the right. I shimmied sideways on my crutches.

When I reached for the switch, I lost my balance. Glen jumped over to steady me.

Carrie made a strange, terrified sound.

I twisted around to see what was wrong with Carrie, but I couldn't see her in the dark garage.

I kept thinking, *Where is she? Did something carry her away?* Then I did the only thing that I knew would help. I prayed, *Jesus, this is all my fault. They were just trying to help me—please keep Carrie safe! Help me find her quickly.*

My prayer was answered almost immediately. I heard Carrie. She was only inches from me. Muffled noises seemed to be coming from her. I thought they were further cries of fear.

But I was wrong. She was laughing.

"I'm sorry." She giggled. "I was 'attacked' by a stuffed animal that fell off a shelf. If there really were an alien life-form in here, I guess we'd all be middle-school stew by now."

She oriented herself in the darkness and reached for the light switch. But when she flipped it, nothing happened.

"Conner, the light didn't come on," she said.

"It must be turned off at the pull chain."

"No problem," Glen said. He felt his way to the center of the garage. He and I had turned the light on in here lots of times in the dark. It just took a little luck. We couldn't see him, but we could hear Glen leap into the air to grab the pull chain. His sneakers smacked the concrete floor several times.

I could tell he'd come close at least once. The metal chain swung against the lightbulb making a tinkling sound each time it hit. After about seven tries Glen caught the chain. He yelled, "All right!" as he pulled down.

A dim blue light filled the garage.

"Nice light," Carrie said.

"We usually have a bright bulb in there. Aunt Bergen must have changed it to that blue one," I answered. The new bulb did not give much light.

But we could see that the garage was full of unusual shapes covered by black cloths.

"It feels weird in here. Let's go back to the house," Glen said.

"No way," Carrie said, ever the mystery solver. "I want to see what's under these mysterious black covers." She walked over to one of the shapes.

"Don't touch it!" I warned, but Carrie had already pulled on its cover. The cloth tumbled to the floor. Something metal reflected the dim blue light and then began to fall.

I watched as a sword seemed to aim itself right at me. Glen dived behind a hanging black cloth, and Carrie jumped sideways, out of the way.

I was certain the sword would hit me. As it fell, I wondered how bad my injuries would be. But when it hit, I didn't feel a thing. Confused, I watched as Carrie reached toward me. She had a funny look on her face.

"Instead of skewering you, that sword collapsed on itself," she said. "I guess it's some sort of trick. If you ask me, this whole place is a trap. What could Aunt Bergen be up to? Who is she, really? Or should I ask, *What* is she?"

We both heard a muffled cry for help. Glen!

"It sounds like he's over there behind that black curtain," I said.

"That's where I saw him dive when the sword fell," Carrie answered. "Let's go help him out."

We pulled back the curtain. And found an empty, upright box.

"Glen?" Carrie called out. "Where are you?"

Glen's muffled voice answered, "Help! Get me out, please."

"We're trying," I told him.

As I turned back to Carrie, I started to lose my balance. I let the curtain fall closed as I steadied myself on my friend's arm.

"What should we do now, Carrie?" I asked.

"Remember, the sword was a fake? Maybe he's stuck behind a false back in the box. That's where his voice seemed to come from. Maybe we can find a way in," Carrie suggested.

She pulled the curtain back to see what kind of tools we needed to free her brother. We were surprised to discover Glen standing in front of us.

Carrie was so shocked that she let the curtain fall closed again.

"Whoa!" said a muffled voice.

"Let's get him out of there," I said.

I pulled the curtain open and reached out a hand to my friend.

Glen was gone again.

"Conner, where did he go?" Carrie asked, sounding a little panicked. "We've got to get him out of there."

I faintly heard Glen say, "Close the curtain." I let the curtain drop again.

I watched as Glen's arm reached around the edge of the dark cloth. I grabbed it and pulled him out of the box.

Glen smiled at us. "Boy, am I glad to be out of there. Every time you closed the curtain, the inner chamber spun around and took me with it," he said.

I glanced at my watch and discovered we'd been in the garage longer than I'd thought. I said to my friends, "We really need to clean up this mess and get out of here. Aunt Bergen could be home any minute now."

We started to straighten up, putting stuff back where it belonged, when Carrie called out, "Does the sword go under this cover?"

"I guess," I answered. I didn't even look. I should have. She had the wrong black cloth in her hand.

As Carrie lifted its corner and peeled it back, something crashed against the side of the box beneath it.

"Wow! What is that?" she said as she jumped back.

Glen and I dropped what we were doing and went to investigate.

"What did you see?" Glen asked.

"I don't really know. When I pulled the corner up, something seemed to jump in this box," she answered.

"It's probably nothing," I said, not really wanting to see what else Aunt Bergen had hidden out here.

"Let's uncover it and see what's there," Glen suggested.

After a moment, I said boldly, "All right." I didn't want to look like a chicken.

We pulled the cover off and discovered a black box. The box had holes drilled all along its sides and top.

The moment the blue light hit the box, something charged the side nearest me. The box rocked, and I jumped back. Glen caught me so I wouldn't fall.

In a slightly shaky voice, Glen said, "Let's just cover it back up and get out of here."

"Good idea," I said. We grabbed the black cloth from the floor. We were ready to drop it on the box when something inside slammed itself against the top. We watched the top of the box bow out.

The creature smashed again, and this time it let out a loud roar. My heart was in my mouth as the box bowed and creaked.

"This box won't take another blow like that. You two get out of here while I cover it," I told Glen and Carrie.

Neither one argued with me. But before either could move, we saw long, pointy claws reaching through the holes on the side of the box.

Instead of running, my friends stood rooted to the floor, staring in fascination.

I called to them, "Carrie, Glen, you've got to help me."

That seemed to bring them out of their trance.

I grabbed the end of the cover and began to pull it toward me. Carrie saw what I had in mind and scurried to help me—my crutches and fear made me awkward.

Glen quickly caught on and grabbed another corner of the cloth. Together, we pulled it over the box. Almost miraculously, the growls and ramming ceased.

"I think it's over," I whispered.

"Let's get out of here," Carrie whispered back.

"Sounds like a plan to me. Let's make sure everything is back where it belongs first."

When we were satisfied that Aunt Bergen wouldn't be able to tell we'd been in the garage, we scooted out the door.

"The light," I said, as I hobbled toward the house. "We forgot to turn out the light!"

Carrie ran back and slipped her hand inside the door to flip the light switch. Whew! We were safe.

Back in the kitchen, I offered my friends a drink. As I poured juice, we heard strange moans drifting up from the basement.

"Is that the sound you told us about?" Glen asked, his eyes wide.

"Yes. What does it sound like to you?" I asked, hoping that he would have a simple answer. But I wasn't ready for the one I got.

"I once heard sounds like that in a horror movie," he answered. "Do you remember, Carrie?"

"Yes, but those moans don't sound like what I heard. Conner, why don't we just go down and check things out?"

"I want to," I told her. "But look what happened in the garage. I don't want to take another chance like that. Besides, stairs are really hard to handle with this cast and those things," I added, pointing at my crutches.

But Glen wanted to explore. He reached for the knob on the basement stairs door.

"I don't think you should go down there. I have the feeling Aunt Bergen is hiding something scary," I told him.

"Maybe the noises are some alien plot to trick you into going to the basement," Carrie added.

Before we could decide what to do, we heard the front door open.

"Conner!" Aunt Bergen called.

I jumped. We couldn't let my aunt know that we were even near the basement door.

"Quick, sit down at the table. Aunt Bergen's got to believe that we just came out here to have something to eat."

I shoved Glen and Carrie toward the kitchen table. We each grabbed a cookie from the full plate sitting there.

Aunt Bergen fairly staggered into the room with her arms full of bags. She looked our way, dropped everything . . . and hurled herself toward us.

18

"Don't eat those!" Aunt Bergen yelled as she ripped the cookie from my hand. Glen and Carrie let their cookies drop to the table.

"Aunt Bergen," I said with surprise. "Why did you do that?"

Maybe she had put poison in the cookies and didn't want Glen and his sister to eat them. Maybe she was saving them for me and my parents.

Aunt Bergen said, "I'm sorry I yelled at you, honey. I made those this morning out of flour, water, and salt. When they're hard enough, I'm going to hang them on the Christmas tree. They'll taste terrible."

I wasn't sure I believed her, but I had to admit that she came up with an explanation quickly.

Aunt Bergen began to bustle around her pile of bags. "I think I'll put this stuff upstairs until I have time to deal with it. You kids have fun," she said with a twinkle.

She picked up most of her purchases and headed to the guest room on the second floor.

Glen quietly said to me, "I think we better go now."

He and Carrie were going to leave me just when I needed them to stay close. "You don't have to go yet. We could play a game or something," I practically begged.

"No, we probably should get home before Mom calls to see if we're still alive," Glen said.

"We'll call you later to see if you are," Carrie added.

"Alive?" I asked.

"That's what I mean," she said.

I walked Glen and Carrie toward the front door. I felt as though I were watching the crew abandon a sinking ship.

After they left, I slipped back into my parents' bedroom in the hope that Aunt Bergen would leave me alone. I left the door open a crack to give me a view of the hallway. Then I settled onto the bed.

Several minutes passed as I nervously watched the hallway. Finally I prayed for awhile to calm myself. I knew God would keep me safe. I picked up my Bible and began to read. After about fifteen minutes, I felt my eyelids begin to droop. I had barely closed them when I heard a scratching noise in the hallway.

At first I didn't want to believe what I saw. A red elf cap bounced past, heading for the front door. And beneath that cap was one of Santa's elves.

I didn't believe in elves or Santa Claus. But I know I saw an elf in my house.

A minute later a green-clad Santa's helper bounced by. Then another one skipped down the hallway.

I heard Aunt Bergen say a cheery good-bye each time an elf left. What was going on? Where had these elves come from?

I crawled out of bed and moved across the thick carpet in my parents' room. Through the partially open door, I saw Aunt Bergen cross the hall, heading to the kitchen. I dragged my cast, trying not to make a noise. I wanted to surprise her.

If I opened the door and caught her with a bunch of elves, would she wipe me out right then?

If Aunt Bergen really was from out of this world, she could probably zap me with some kind of laser beam. I had to be careful.

I reached for the door and stopped. I closed my eyes to say a prayer, took a deep breath, and prepared myself.

Before I could reach for the door, it flew open.

"There you are!" Aunt Bergen said. "I wondered where you'd gotten to. Have your friends gone home?" Her words snapped me to attention.

"Uh, yes. I was just coming out to see about all the noise in the hallway. What's going on out here?" I tried to smile so she wouldn't think that I had seen the elves.

She tousled my hair. She said, "Nothing to worry yourself about."

"But I really want to know," I said emphatically.

"All right then. Santa's little helpers have been helping me out." Aunt Bergen giggled, then turned around and headed back down the hallway. Over her shoulder, she said, "I've got a number of things to attend to. If you need anything, let me know."

"Actually, I need some stuff from my room, but I'll go up and get it. It will probably take me a few minutes," I said as she walked away.

From the living room, she answered, "That's fine, honey."

My cast wasn't easy to drag up all those steps. I was out of breath by the time I made it to the top. Exhausted, I dropped onto my bed. Then I rolled over to grab my phone. I needed to tell Glen what had just happened to see what he thought. I could hear Aunt Bergen moving around downstairs.

The phone rang three times before Glen picked it up. "Hello?" he answered.

"Hi, it's Conner," I said. "I just saw the strangest thing."

"That's nothing new for your house lately," he joked.

"This isn't funny," I reminded him. "I came all the way upstairs just to call you. I need to tell someone what I saw before it's too late for me to tell anybody anything."

"Go ahead. I'll even write it down in case something does happen to you," Glen said.

"Well, I was lying in bed in my parents' room," I explained. "The door was open a little, and I saw all these Santa-type elves walk down the hall. Aunt Bergen talked to them like they were old friends. It was really weird."

Glen was quiet on the other end of the line. I could hear the scratch of pencil on paper. He really was writing it down. I guess he realized how serious my situation was becoming. Then I heard his mother's voice in the background.

"I've got to go," he told me. "I'll call you later." Then he hung up.

I made my way into the hallway. I wondered where Aunt Bergen was and called her name. No answer. I was definitely alone on the second floor.

I had a chance to search her room, and I intended to take it.

But something pricked my conscience. Snooping around in someone's room was disrespectful. And I had always been taught to honor and respect my elders.

I thought for a moment, then rationalized, *But what if this is really some outer-space alien?* I had to go for it.

I snuck into our small guest bedroom. I wasn't sure what I might find there—I didn't even know what to look for. What would a space alien have in her bedroom? A secret decoder ring?

My cast and crutches made it hard to slip around smoothly and quietly, but I had to be as silent as possible. The room had a closet, a bed, and a dresser. At the foot of the bed was an old chest that Mom kept blankets in.

I went to the dresser first. I pulled open the drawers

and quickly looked inside. Nothing out of the ordinary caught my attention. I finished with the drawers and started to turn away.

Then I noticed a picture frame lying facedown on top of the dresser. I flipped it over. It couldn't be . . .

Aunt Bergen was floating in the air on her back. Nothing held her up.

A man was standing beside her with his arms in the air. I figured he had to be Uncle Charlie, her husband who had died. Was he making her float?

That picture was enough proof for me. Normal people simply don't float in the air. I knew I couldn't keep the picture, but I had to show it to somebody else. I decided to call Glen and get him to come over again.

Before I left Aunt Bergen's room, though, I wanted to peek in the closet. I guessed that's where she'd keep her radio beam transmitter or whatever odd devices she had.

I began to pull the closet door open. It squeaked. That made me nervous. I couldn't let Aunt Bergen catch me. If she really was some kind of alien, I needed time to foil her plan of taking over my family.

I gently pulled a little more on the door. It surprised me by swinging open easily.

Something huge and dressed in a black hood fell out of the closet.

I stumbled backward and landed flat on my back on the bed, pinned by the mysterious form.

I struggled to get away. I punched and pulled, but the thing stayed with me. The harder I struggled, the tighter it seemed to hold me.

Finally, I gave up and relaxed. Then I got a good look at it. It was only Aunt Bergen's black-hooded cape wrapped around a dress form. I had gotten tangled up in the cloth. Laughing at myself, I pulled myself free. Then I walked over to the closet to see what else might give me cardiac problems.

The only thing I found was a suitcase pushed as far back in the corner as possible. That looked suspicious to me. I tried to reach it, but my cast prevented me from getting close enough.

I had a brilliant idea. I could use one of my crutches to hook the suitcase's handle and pull it out of the corner. I carefully aimed the tip of the crutch. Success on my first try! I slowly dragged the suitcase within reach.

My heart was beating hard. This suitcase might

hold the answers to all my questions. I had to get it open before Aunt Bergen came looking for me and caught me.

As I popped open the latches, the phone rang.

I almost panicked. I knew I had to get out of Aunt Bergen's room quickly. If the call was for me, she'd come searching for me. I couldn't let her find me in her room.

The suitcase would have to wait.

I reclosed the latches and slid the bag back into the closet. I pushed the door shut and hobbled into the hall.

I wanted to get downstairs to find out who had called. But first I stopped in my room to pick up a couple of books. I didn't want Aunt Bergen to wonder what I'd been doing upstairs. I slipped the books into my backpack and put it on, so my hands were free to guide my crutches.

The trip down took less time and energy than the trip up. When I arrived at the bottom, I decided to slip into Mom and Dad's room. I didn't want Aunt Bergen to hear me and come rushing in, so I tried to be very quiet. The bedroom door was open. As I got closer to it, I heard Aunt Bergen in my parents' bathroom. She was singing "Have Yourself a Merry Little Christmas" while she cleaned.

The phone call must have been for her. I wondered if other aliens had called to find out about Aunt

74

Bergen's progress in taking over my family. How long did I have before they'd invade our house?

I looked in the bedroom. There he was again—sitting on the bed like he owned it!

I glanced at his eyes. I was sure Boris would wink at me again.

I spun around as quickly as my cast and crutches would let me. I didn't want to climb the mountain of stairs again, but I needed to in order to carry out my idea.

When I got to the top, I hobbled to my room to catch my breath. Those stairs were hard work. Then I came out of my room and closed the door loudly to get Aunt Bergen's attention. I called down, "Aunt Bergen, I'm heading down now. If you hear something crash, it's just me falling."

But she didn't answer.

I called again. Still no answer.

She must have finished cleaning in the bathroom and gone somewhere else while I was in my bedroom.

I was too tired to walk the steps again, so I pushed my crutches down the stairs and slid down the banister. When I hit bottom, I picked up my crutches and hobbled to the bedroom, expecting Boris to be sitting on the bed. He wasn't.

Where did he go? I asked myself. Dummies don't get up and walk away, do they? He had to be nearby. I was sure that if I found Aunt Bergen, I would also find Boris.

I shifted my clumsy cast around and guided myself down the hall.

"Aunt Bergen," I called. The house was silent.

Maybe she'd gone outside. If she had, I was alone in the house. That meant the basement was waiting for me.

I was finally getting better at moving around with one leg in a cast. I reached the basement door in no time.

I stopped and called for Aunt Bergen again. When I was sure she wasn't around, my heart started thumping hard. The idea of finally finding out what lurked in my basement had me pretty nervous. Even my breath came in short gasps. I murmured to myself, "Here goes nothing."

When I reached over to grab the doorknob, my left crutch slipped from my hand and fell toward the wood door. I jerked my arm toward it and grabbed at it like an acrobat grabs a trapeze bar.

But it was too late. It had made contact. The noise echoed loudly in the kitchen.

I stood absolutely still and listened hard. No sign of Aunt Bergen. Good.

Then a faint sound came from the other side of the

basement door. I heard long nails scratching at the wood. Low moaning joined the scratching sound.

I couldn't do it. I couldn't make myself open the door. I was so scared my teeth started chattering.

"God's perfect love takes away fear; God's perfect love takes away fear," I repeated to myself under my breath. First John 4:18 had given me courage before, and I really needed it now.

The only thing that kept me from the unknown was the basement door.

What was on the other side? Someone Aunt Bergen had captured? Even though I was scared, I had to find out. It might be my last chance to help whoever it was. If I waited, it might be too late. Whatever Aunt Bergen had in mind for me, she wasn't going to wait forever.

My parents would be coming home soon. I wondered if she'd try to get me out of the way before then, so she could focus on them.

I reached again for the doorknob. The scratching had stopped. Whoever or whatever was in the basement was waiting for me. I *had* to see what it was. I had to be brave.

"Conner!" Aunt Bergen's voice stopped me cold. It sounded like she was upstairs. "Conner, where did you go?"

I couldn't let her know that I had tried to get into the basement again. I looked around for a place to hide.

Then I realized there was a good place outside. The sliding glass door to the patio was only a few feet away. I could slip out before she came downstairs.

Hobbling quickly to the door, I slid it open. I grabbed a coat from the pegs beside the door. Right outside was the picnic table. I dropped onto the seat and slipped into my coat. When Aunt Bergen found me, I wanted her to think I'd just come out for a bit of fresh air.

I smiled to myself because I liked my plan. Then an arm fell across my shoulder.

I snapped my head around and found myself looking straight into Boris's eyes.

I scrambled to my feet and spoke softly to him. "Listen here, pal. I know what's going on around this place. The two of you are planning to eliminate my family so your space alien buddies can invade our bodies.

"Well, you can just forget about it because God's Spirit, who is in me, is greater than the devil, who is out in the world," I said, paraphrasing 1 John 4:4 slightly. "I'm onto your plan. I've already called the cops, and they'll be here in a few minutes. So don't try anything funny."

Boris stared back at me and then slumped a little. His arms lifted in the air as he sank against the picnic table. He was surrendering.

I must be going nuts. I was threatening a dummy.

What was even crazier was that the dummy seemed to be surrendering peacefully.

"Just stay right there, you termite feast. Don't come any closer!"

My words fell on deaf ears. He slid down farther.

81

Then he fell to his side onto the seat with his face buried in his hands.

He didn't move. I imagined he was filled with remorse. Because of that, I changed the way I spoke to him.

"I'm sorry I spoke so harshly to you. But you have to understand that since you and Aunt Bergen moved in, my life has been filled with bizarre stuff. I need some answers. Are you willing to answer some questions?"

He made no movement. I pushed Boris a little. He toppled to the wood deck with a thump. His eyes closed.

Oh, no! If Aunt Bergen hadn't decided whether to get rid of me yet, I just helped her do so. Had I killed Boris?

Aunt Bergen would most likely let the creature scratching in the basement have me. It would use its long, pointed nails to turn me into dinner.

If Aunt Bergen was really a space alien like Glen said, she could do just about anything to me. All the possible horrors waiting for me flashed before my eyes.

Aunt Bergen's voice broke into my thoughts. It sounded like she was calling my name out the front door.

Good! I should have enough time to slip back inside. The sliding glass door opened with my tug.

I heard the front door close as I tumbled back into the kitchen.

"Conner!" she called.

"I'm right here, Aunt Bergen," I answered.

She entered the kitchen. She had a puzzled look in her eyes. "I've been looking all over for you," she said. "I was so worried. Didn't you hear me calling?"

"I'm sorry if I scared you," I told her. I wished she was sorry she scared *me* too.

"I have so many plans for taking care of your family on Christmas Day," she said. "Maybe I should practice a few on you."

She smiled. But I had a feeling her plans might not be much fun for me.

The time was getting too close. I was sure she wanted to get rid of me before I had a chance to warn my parents about her.

She was planning to take care of them on Christmas Day. Somehow I had to survive. I just had to warn my parents.

"Exactly what are you going to do to me?" I asked, even though I really didn't want to know.

"Well, I thought I would start with—"

The ring of the telephone interrupted her.

She hurried to the phone in the living room. Did she want some privacy to hatch her plot? I had to know. I reached for the extension in the kitchen.

We picked up our receivers at the same time. "Hello," we both said at the same time.

"Hi, Conner. Hi, Aunt Bergen. How are things at home?" a wonderful voice asked.

Mom was on the line!

"Just fine, dear," Aunt Bergen said. "Conner and I are having a great time."

Mom needed to know what was in our future. With Aunt Bergen on the other phone, I couldn't say a word—at least not a direct word.

But I had an idea. Maybe I could send my message by stressing certain words. It was worth a try. Anything was worth a try.

"I sure *miss* everybody, Mom," I said. "Aunt Bergen's about to *kill* me. Her jokes really *choke* me up."

"That's great, Conner. Aunt Bergen, thanks for taking such good care of him," Mom said.

She hadn't gotten the message. My code didn't work. I had to try harder.

I jumped in again. "Her jokes will just *slay* me."

"My goodness, Aunt Bergen, I've never heard Conner so happy to have someone staying with him before. We should have you over more often," Mom said.

She still didn't get it.

Maybe I needed to be more direct. "I sure miss everyone, Mom. When are you coming home? I'm *dying* to have you come home."

"Well, that's why I called. There's a pretty heavy snowstorm headed our way. We aren't sure if the plane will get out on time. We may be here for an extra day," she told us.

Panic set in. "You can't. I'll *die* if you don't get home soon." I meant it too.

"You're being a little dramatic, don't you think? You've been away at camp longer than this. We'll be home before Christmas," Mom said.

I heard someone talking in the background.

"I have to go now. Your dad and I love you, honey. And thanks again, Aunt Bergen. Bye," she said. She hung up the phone.

I put the receiver down and turned to see Aunt Bergen walking into the kitchen toward me.

She looked around for a moment.

Then she reached over and picked up Mom's largest knife.

"Aunt Bergen, I was only kidding on the phone. I could stay here forever with you," I pleaded.

"That's nice, Conner." She smiled.

"I feel like going for a walk. I think I'll step out for a minute." I fumbled out the words. I needed an excuse that would carry me away from my aunt, and the knife.

"I'm afraid I can't let you do that," she answered. Aunt Bergen took two steps toward me.

I couldn't believe it would all be over so soon, I thought to myself. *This stinks. This really stinks.*

"Why don't you go rest in the living room for a bit? I'll have things ready for you in a few minutes." She smiled again.

"Things?" I blurted out. "Do you call what you're going to do *things?*"

"My goodness, there's no reason to get so upset. I do this all the time. As you kids say, 'It's no big deal.' I'll come get you when everything is ready," Aunt Bergen said.

I quickly hobbled off. Instead of going to the living room, I decided to barricade myself in my parents' room.

I wondered what Aunt Bergen had planned. She could release the creature moaning in the basement. She could let Boris creep into my room. Or she could . . .

I had to protect myself. I would build a trap for anyone who tried to enter the room.

I had to work fast; I knew I didn't have much time.

In the bathroom I found a long-handled brush for washing your back. I balanced the handle on the doorknob. If anyone opened the door, the brush would fall to the floor and alert me. Then I realized it would make a noise, but it wouldn't protect me.

I looked carefully around the room and noticed that the dresser was in the perfect position. I could set something on its top that was long enough to reach the door. If the brush fell, it would hit that something and send it into the air. I wondered what to use. Then it came to me.

Hanging on a hook in the closet was a long shoehorn. I gave it to Dad last Christmas. I had no idea if he ever used it, but I sure could. Holding the long shoehorn in my teeth, I propelled myself back to the door on my crutches. I carefully positioned the shoehorn on the end of the dresser. Then I grabbed Mom's big bath puff, which was drenched with powder. I carefully placed it on the part of the shoe-horn that sat on the dresser.

The falling brush would strike the end of the shoe-horn that stuck over the edge of the dresser. The powder-filled puff would fly into the air and smack any intruder in the face. In all the commotion, I could get away safely.

I scanned the room again, satisfied.

Feeling fairly safe, I curled up on the bed. The day had worn me out. As I relaxed, I closed my eyes. I did not realize I had fallen asleep until I woke up and discovered the sun had gone down. At first, I didn't know where I was. I heard noises. I didn't know if they were part of a dream or real.

"Conner, it's time," Aunt Bergen said from the other side of the door.

"Wh . . . what?" I slurred.

"I said it's time. I'm ready for you to come out now," she said.

"I'll be right there," I said. I swung my legs around and lowered them to the floor.

My head felt like it had goo in it. I couldn't think.

It was dark, and I forgot about the brush on the doorknob. I reached out to open the door and knocked the brush down. It crashed onto the shoehorn, and the powdery puff smacked me on the side of my head.

White dust fairly blinded me. When I sucked in air in surprise, a few bits of the white powder rushed up my nose.

It tickled. A hurricane-force sneeze was about to come. "Ah-h-h-h choo-o-o!"

The windows and the door rattled.

"Are you all right, Conner?" Aunt Bergen asked.

"Yes, I'm fine. I just sneezed. I'll be out in a minute."

"Take your time. I'll meet you in the kitchen," she told me.

I tried to wipe the powder off, but it was hopeless. When I got to the kitchen, Aunt Bergen stared at me.

She lowered her eyebrows as if she was trying to think of a question.

Then Aunt Bergen began to giggle.

"You look like a ghost. Should I get the feather duster and dust you off?" she asked.

"No, I'm fine," I said. I didn't want to have to explain the powder, so even though I didn't want to know, I asked, "What do you have waiting for me?"

"It's something very special," she told me.

The phone rang.

Aunt Bergen lifted the receiver. She did not say much, but when she hung up the phone, her face was beaming.

"This will have to wait. A surprise has come in at the bus station. I need to call a cab and get down there right away," she said.

The cab arrived in less than ten minutes.

As I watched Aunt Bergen leave, I wondered, *Who in the world is at the bus station? Or what?*

Suddenly I remembered that I wanted to go check out the basement. I had made it about halfway across the kitchen floor when the doorbell rang.

I turned around and hobbled toward the door slowly. I was getting good at moving the extra weight of my cast.

The doorbell rang again. Whoever was waiting seemed pretty impatient.

When I pulled open the front door, a blast of snow

blew into my face. The icy particles blinded me for an instant. Before I could wipe the snow from my face, the delivery man thrust a box at me, wished me a "Merry Christmas," and ran back to his truck.

It looked like the snowstorm had picked up. I slammed the door to keep more snow from blowing into the house.

The package wasn't for me, so I left it near the front door. I didn't have time to place it under the Christmas tree. I wanted to get to the basement.

The walk back to the kitchen seemed to take forever. Or maybe it seemed so long because my arms had gotten very tired.

When my cast hit the linoleum floor, I heard another ring—the telephone. The whole world knew that I was up to something important. Everyone seemed determined to stop me.

I picked up the phone and said, "Hello."

"Conner, it's me, Glen."

"I know it's you. What do you want?" I fired at him.

"I was calling to see if you are still a member of the human race—or have you become a space alien?" he quizzed.

"That's a silly question," I said. "If I were an alien, do you think I would tell you? You should ask me something that only I would know."

"Like what?" he asked.

"That's another silly question. If I tell you what to

ask me, I would already have the answer. You need to ask a question that you know the answer to," I told him.

"I get it," he said. "Here's my question. What did I have for breakfast this morning?"

"Glen, the question needs to be something that we both know the answer to," I said. I was getting frustrated with him.

"Conner, I don't need some silly question to know it's you. Nobody else could get all worked up about something like a question. You must be you." Glen laughed.

"Thanks for the call, Glen. I'll see you later. Right now, I've got to get into the basement to see what Aunt Bergen is hiding," I told him. "I'll talk to you later."

I hopped the few steps toward the basement door. I would finally find out who, or what, was down there—and why.

I twisted the knob to pull the door open.

And the front door blew open with a crash.

Aunt Bergen yelled, "Help!"

"Come quickly, Conner. I need your help to get this thing inside," she called urgently.

I hobbled down the hall, watching the snow blow all around her. She was pushing a box into the hall and trying to close the door behind her. By the time I reached her, the door was nearly closed.

"I can't wait for you to see what I have inside this box. Unfortunately, you'll have to wait until your parents come home," she said. She smiled again.

"Can you give me a little hint?" I asked.

"Oh, I can't do that. I want it to be a big surprise for everyone. But I do have something waiting for you in the kitchen. Come with me, young man. I'll show you the thing I do that some people would die for," she told me.

So this was it. This was the end. I wished I could have warned my folks.

I thought about everything that had happened.

Strange elves had skipped through the house.

A creepy dummy waited on the patio.

A killer beast had tried to escape its box in our garage.

And a mysterious creature moaned in the basement.

What is she up to, Lord? I prayed. *Please stay by my side.*

She followed me down the hall, guiding me into the kitchen. Then she stood directly in front of me and held out a cloth. "I want you to blindfold yourself," she said.

My stomach did flips, and my mouth went dry. After I put the blindfold on, Aunt Bergen made me sit on a swivel bar stool. She turned me around and around until I was dizzy. I was thoroughly confused.

Then she stopped me.

"Are you sure you can't see?" she asked.

I nodded. Actually, I was so scared that I honestly didn't want to see.

"Now lean forward," she said.

I didn't know what to do. I was scared, but I couldn't run. Even if I could get to the door, the elves were probably waiting outside.

I'd never felt so trapped.

She again told me to lean forward. This time, she gently pushed on the back of my head. I drew in a breath and said another prayer.

Then it hit me.

Aunt Bergen had spent her day making my favorite meal! I recognized the smell of spaghetti sauce with meatballs. She had also made cheese ravioli. *Mmmm.*

"Aunt Bergen, how did you know this was my favorite?" I asked with surprise as she took off my blindfold.

"Your mother left me a list of things I could do to get your mind off having to stay here. This was one of them. Sit down and eat up. You never know if you'll ever have another meal again." She giggled out the words.

What did she mean by that? Was this my last meal? Had she poisoned it? I really didn't want to find out. But with Aunt Bergen watching me intently, I felt like I had to taste it.

It was as good as it smelled!

We had almost finished eating dinner when we heard a loud hammering outside.

"Finally! I thought they would never get here," Aunt Bergen said. She hurried down the hallway and ran out the front door.

There was no way I could keep up with her. I started hobbling after her to see what was going on. As I reached the front door, it burst open and Aunt Bergen fairly danced back inside. She wore a mischievous smile.

"What's all the noise?" I asked, puzzled.

"I've asked some workers to take care of something out front," she answered.

I wanted more information than that.

"What kind of something?" I asked.

"The kind that will make people want to come to your house," Aunt Bergen said, then she giggled.

I'd already figured out that she giggled only when she had something up her sleeve.

Before I could ask another question, she hurried me back down the hall to finish our meal.

My head was swimming. I needed my parents to come home now. The rest of the evening I wondered how I could keep my folks safe. The elves had to be hiding somewhere outside. I didn't want Mom and Dad to fall into some sort of trap. I was afraid they'd join the creature moaning in the basement.

I was still thinking the problem over as I got ready for bed. But before I could come up with a good plan, I drifted off to sleep. A strange noise from the living room partially woke me. I wasn't sure what it was.

I listened carefully and eventually recognized it. Someone was using Mom's rocking chair.

That rocking chair had belonged to my mom's grandmother. It was beautiful but fragile. A skilled craftsperson had made it out of dark wood and had carved ornate scrollwork on it. My grandmother had made its needlepoint cushion. It was Mom's favorite antique. She rocked in it all the time, but she didn't like anyone else to use it. She was afraid it would get broken.

I guess Aunt Bergen didn't know she shouldn't sit in it. I thought about getting out of bed to tell her. Then I decided I was too comfortable to get up.

Above me I heard footsteps. Aunt Bergen must be in the guest bedroom getting ready for bed. I could track her movements by the sound of her steps.

I suddenly felt a chill.

If Aunt Bergen's upstairs, then who's in the rocking chair?

I struggled out from under the covers. Throwing my legs over the side of the bed, I reached for my crutches and headed for the bedroom door. I had to see who, or what, was in Mom's favorite chair.

I moved quietly into the hallway. I could still hear Aunt Bergen walking around upstairs.

I peered into the room. The rocking chair stood out of my sight, but I could see a partial reflection of it in a mirror across the room.

I should have been able to see a pair of feet moving the chair. But the chair seemed to be rocking by itself.

How was it moving? Was some invisible being pushing it? My breath came out in short bursts. I was extremely frightened.

What was I about to come face to face with?

The truth suddenly dawned on me. I was looking at the chair in a mirror. I'd read that certain creatures did not reflect in mirrors. I had always laughed at stuff like that. But now I wasn't so sure. Maybe aliens from outer space didn't reflect in mirrors.

My body tensed. The sound of beating wings was coming straight at me. Had the creature turned into a bat?

27

What could possibly be flying around our house in the middle of the night?

I threw my arms up to protect my face as the creature flew at me. I closed my eyes tight as I heard something veer away from me and head out the doorway.

I stood there stunned. It took me a few minutes to get my breathing back to normal. Had I just faced some evil friend of Aunt Bergen? What should I do?

Then I heard Aunt Bergen's voice. I thought she said, "Elvira, there you are. You've been gone a while. Were you out looking for dinner? You know you can have as much as you want from downstairs later. Until then, I have a sweet treat for you in my room."

She had to be talking to the flying creature. She had called it Elvira. I thought I should get back to my folks' bedroom before Elvira decided she wanted something bigger for her midnight snack.

In my hurry to find some place safe, I knocked over a chair with a crutch. It fell with a loud crash. I leaned over to pick it up but lost my balance. It took a few seconds to right myself. I realized I would have to calm down to regain my coordination. I stood up and took a few deep breaths.

When I finally reached out to set the chair back up, something gripped my hand from behind me.

28

As the hand curled its bony fingers around my arm, I screamed and jerked away.

Nothing was going to take me that easily. I tensed my body against an attack.

Before I could turn around, I heard, "I'm sorry. Did I startle you again?"

"Aunt Bergen!" I said with a mixture of surprise, joy, and fear.

"I heard something crash down here. I hoped it wasn't one of my little friends doing some kind of mischief. I can see that it wasn't," she said as she smiled at me.

Aunt Bergen helped me set the chair up. I told her, "Thanks. I didn't mean to disturb you."

"Oh, that's okay. I was just taking care of some last-minute things before my big surprise for your family on Christmas. But it's late. We'd better get to bed. Tomorrow is going to be a big day," she told me.

I said goodnight and headed back to bed. At that

103

point, only Glen, Carrie, and I knew her secret. It was too late to call them tonight. First thing tomorrow I had to warn them about the latest developments.

The next morning, hammering outside woke me. The workers had returned to our yard. I wondered what they were building, but Aunt Bergen wouldn't let me go outside to look.

The phone rang.

"Hi, Conner. This is Glen and Carrie's mom. Can I talk to Glen?" she asked.

"He's not here," I told her.

"That's odd. I thought the kids were headed to your house. Maybe they went sledding in the churchyard instead," she mused. "Well, if they do show up, please have Glen call home. In the meantime, I'll make a few more phone calls."

I stared at the phone, convinced. Aunt Bergen had Glen and Carrie!

I was afraid for my friends. What if they met the same fate as the thing moaning in the basement? Maybe Aunt Bergen figured out that we were onto her plan. I tried not to let my fear show as I assured their mother that I'd tell them to call her if I saw them.

"And, Conner," she said, "that thing the workers are building in your front yard is amazing. I can't wait to see your parents' reaction. I'll bet your mom will be tickled when she sees it." She chuckled a good-bye and hung up.

How could she laugh at a time like this? But then, I guess she didn't realize my alien aunt had abducted her children.

After I hung up the phone, the house seemed pretty quiet. I could hear Aunt Bergen humming a Christmas carol in the kitchen.

I hobbled toward the kitchen. Aunt Bergen had a strange smile on her face. Then she took a step to the right and revealed a stack of pancakes covered in syrup waiting for me on the table.

"I thought I'd make you a special breakfast. I hope you like syrup," she said, placing the bottle near my plate.

"Well, thanks, Aunt Bergen. I really appreciate it," I told her. But I kept my guard up.

Had she done something with my friends? Was I living in a very real horror movie?

Aunt Bergen strolled across the kitchen floor and grabbed a basket of clean, folded clothes. As she left the kitchen, she called back over her shoulder, "I'm going to put these clothes away and tidy up my room. If the workers out front need anything, feel free to call me. But don't peek outside."

I rotated my cast-covered leg under the table and sat down to eat my pancakes.

They tasted great. I had to admit that Aunt Bergen had turned out to be a good cook. Then I heard a sound from deep in the basement.

Maybe it was Glen and Carrie!

I was scared, but I knew I had to try and save my friends.

I scooted toward the basement door. I listened for Aunt Bergen. She was still bustling around upstairs.

I felt determined. This time I was going to make it into the basement. I pulled the door open and groped around on the landing, looking for the light switch.

A big, hairy hand clamped down on my shoulder. I was so startled, I almost toppled down the dark stairs groped around in the darkness looking for the light switch.

A big, hairy hand clamped down on my shoulder.

I was so startled, I almost toppled down the dark stairs.

"I'm sorry, kid," a deep voice boomed at me. The hairy hand pulled me up by my shirt.

When I had my balance again, he continued, "I knocked on the door, but no one answered. So I let myself in to see if I could rouse somebody. Where can I find some strong rope?"

He must be one of the workers from outside.

"Strong rope? I guess we keep it—" I stopped mid-sentence.

Why is he looking for rope? Do I really want him to have it?

"Well, gosh, I don't know where we keep it." I tried to act cool and collected. "By the way, what are you making out there?" I asked.

I wanted him to think that it was just an idle question. Maybe he would slip up and tell me what was going on.

He smiled at me. "Your aunt told me that you would try to get information out of me. But this is supposed to be a surprise. My kids would just die if we had one of these things in our yard. In fact, I bet they would hang around all the time," he said.

"Uh, right," I said. I didn't really know what to say. This man wanted rope, and he seemed happy that his kids would want to *hang* around. He was almost as creepy as Aunt Bergen could be.

Since I couldn't help him, the worker went back outside. I hobbled to the window next to the front door. I wanted to see what was in the yard.

I pressed my eye against the cold glass and tried to see out. But the window was too frosty. I rubbed it hard to remove the thin ice.

Pushing my eye up to the clear spot, I saw another eye looking back at me. One of the elves was sitting on the other side of the glass just waiting for me. He gave me a little wave and winked at me—just like Boris had.

I felt trapped. My peaceful Christmas season had turned into a season of fright.

I wanted to escape, but I didn't know how.

I needed to find Glen and Carrie and rescue them, but I didn't know how to do that either.

I didn't know what Aunt Bergen was, and I wasn't sure that I wanted to find out. But I couldn't see any way to get free from the house and my aunt.

The house had only three outside doors. If she had someone at all the windows, I bet she also had the doors covered by her little friends. Since I couldn't get out, I needed to find a place to hide.

Where? Where could I go?

The only place I had felt safe since Aunt Bergen had come was in my parents' bedroom. I scooted my weary body there and lay on the floor beside the bed. I slid my crutches under it and then eased my body into the dark dustiness beneath the bed.

I tried to pull my cast completely under with me. But it still stuck out a bit. Aunt Bergen would be able to see me for sure. I slid in a little farther.

I touched something.

A shoe? I recognized the feel of canvas and rubber. I had found a sneaker. I wondered who it belonged to. If it was one of mine, I should toss it out from under the bed. I'd never find it again otherwise.

I pulled on the sneaker to get a better look at it. It felt like it was attached to something.

I turned my head to see what I was dragging toward me.

I had Boris's sneaker in my hand.

And Boris was still wearing it.

I flew out from under the bed as fast as I could, considering I had one leg in a cast.

Grabbing my crutches, I hopped and stumbled my way out of the room.

Aunt Bergen's friends were watching me. Not even my parents' room was safe. No matter where I went, she would know.

I decided to station myself where I could see things coming and going. I wasn't going to get caught by surprise. I headed for the living room. From there I could watch the hallway and the stairs. I sat with my back against the wall and tried to calm my breathing. As I looked around the room, I noticed some new decorations. More unusual ornaments were hanging on the tree. One in particular caught my eye.

Curious, I reached over to touch it. I saw a little red button on its side, so I pushed it. The glass ball opened up. It began to make the most beautiful music.

Wow, I thought. *That's really neat.*

Then I looked closer. Inside I saw a tiny choir. I realized with horror that the singers were real. Somehow Aunt Bergen had trapped a choir inside an ornament!

I was so scared I could barely think.

I pushed myself away from the horror without looking back. I tumbled headlong into a stack of gifts. Boxes scattered all around me. Some were pretty heavy and hurt as they fell on me.

I struggled to stand. Then I heard an odd sound behind me. I had gotten turned around so I couldn't see the doorway.

Still frightened, I slowly looked over my shoulder. Standing in the archway to the living room was a figure dressed in black. A high, pointed black hood covered its head. Two bright eyes shined at me from within the hood.

I gasped.

"Are you all right, Conner?" asked Aunt Bergen's voice.

"I knew you were going to come for me sometime," I said in a panic to the hooded figure. "But I'm not going down without a fight."

She started toward me. What should I do?

My brain took over; I needed to get to the phone. I had to call 911. Someone had to know that an alien posing as a relative dressed in a black cape and hood wanted to get me.

The cops probably wouldn't believe me, but I had to take that chance. Keeping the couch between me and Aunt Bergen, I burst past her. I was glad I'd been practicing on my crutches so much. I focused all my energy on getting to the kitchen phone.

"You're not going to make me disappear, and I'm not going to be carried off by flying aliens," I yelled as I pounded down the hall.

Aunt Bergen had the most confused look on her face.

I hopped to the phone and snatched it from the cradle.

As I started to punch in the numbers, a hand reached out to gently take the receiver from me.

33

I turned. I couldn't believe my eyes.

"What's the matter, Conner?" Mom asked.

"Mom! Dad! You're home! Help me! Save yourself! Aunt Bergen wants to do us in. She's got a space alien friend who flies, and weird little elves guarding the house, and there's some creature in a box in the garage." My words just spilled out.

"What are you talking about? Aunt Bergen doesn't want to hurt you. And there's no creature in the garage," Dad said, looking puzzled.

"I know there is. What's the matter with you? Are you under Aunt Bergen's spell, too? Or are you in on the plan? Maybe I'm the only one who's supposed to disappear." I was babbling. I was upset. I couldn't believe that my own family was willing to let this happen to me.

"What in the world are you talking about?" Mom asked. "Aunt Bergen, has he been like this the whole time?"

117

"I don't understand. I thought Conner and I were having a splendid time. I was even going to use him in my act tomorrow afternoon," she said.

Aunt Bergen stretched out her hand toward me and continued, "Come with me, dear. I'll show you what's in the garage and what the workers have been building in the front yard."

"It's all very nice," my dad added.

"Conner, she's just up to her old tricks," Mom said with an encouraging smile.

I was sure that Aunt Bergen, the alien, had somehow gotten to them. I wasn't sure how, but I knew she had.

"Calm down and tell me what you think is going on," Mom said.

"Aunt Bergen has some kind of beast in a box in the garage. And someone—or something—keeps making the strangest sounds in our basement.

"A creepy dummy named Boris has been following me around. I just know he's watching me for her.

"And the Christmas tree ornaments—somehow she's trapped living people inside them.

"An invisible creature named Elvira was rocking in your antique chair, then it flew upstairs.

"Worst of all, she's done something with Glen and Carrie. Their mom said they came over here and disappeared. I never saw them.

"Aunt Bergen must be some kind of alien to have

118

so much power. The only thing that's kept me safe is prayer. But I was still afraid.

"And I had to live with this fear while you were out on the ski slopes enjoying yourselves," I barreled to a stop.

Mom looked at Aunt Bergen. Aunt Bergen looked at Dad.

Suddenly they all cracked up.

I knew we were in danger, but all they could do was laugh!

Aunt Bergen took a step toward me. I was sure this was the end.

"Conner," she said, "I'm sorry if I scared you. I want you to know that I am *not* an alien."

Mom looked at Dad and nodded. He went to the basement door and pulled it open.

Oh no! I thought. *The creature is going to devour him!*

But Mom and Aunt Bergen didn't seem alarmed at all. When Dad came back up the stairs, he held something wiggly. A puppy! Little black eyes peeked out at me from a thatch of long gray fur.

"You said that you wanted a dog for Christmas. We bought him just before we left. Aunt Bergen was trying to hide him from you so he would be a surprise," Dad told me.

He added, "That's what made the odd sounds in the basement."

"But what about Boris? And what about Glen and

Carrie? I just know you have my friends caged up somewhere. And what was that creature that flew around the house and nearly attacked me?" I challenged anybody to answer me.

"We better sit down. I think it's time for me to tell my story," Aunt Bergen said.

Her eyes twinkled with merriment. "Many years ago Uncle Charlie and I traveled around the United States doing magic shows. We had such fun!" she began.

"Uncle Charlie's favorite illusion was the 'Beast in the Box.' He built a box complete with claws and sound effects—it seemed like a beast was trying to get out. Then he would pop the box open and show everyone it was empty. Kids thought he made the beast disappear."

"Well, that explains the beast in the garage," I said. "But what about Boris?" I asked.

"Boris is my dummy. Long ago I used him in the magic shows. Although I've recently done some church and club meetings with him, I'm afraid I'm a little out of practice. I didn't realize you caught me working on my routine. I've practiced with him several times in the last few days. Whenever I heard you coming, I tried to hide him. I wanted to keep Boris a surprise for later," Aunt Bergen explained.

"Okay, explain what happened to Glen and Carrie. Their mother said that they came over here and disappeared," I challenged again.

"Glen and Carrie are such nice kids. When they came over this morning, you were still asleep. I asked them to run an errand for me. They're probably back home by now.

"By the way, I told them about the magic act. I promised I would do a show for the neighborhood kids after Christmas—on the stage that my friends have been building in the front yard."

I digested that information. "You've explained just about everything but Elvira—and the people trapped in the tree ornaments," I said.

"Oh, yes. Every magician uses a dove. I had Elvira shipped to me; that's what I had to pick up at the bus station. When I got her home, I let her out of her cage to stretch her wings. She must have come downstairs to explore the house."

I smiled. "Well, you can tell her that I saved her life."

Aunt Bergen looked at me, puzzled. "Why?"

"She sat on Mom's antique rocker. I guess I chased her away before she did anything wrong," I joked.

I was slowly beginning to understand. Aunt Bergen wasn't an alien. She was just a little strange.

Aunt Bergen continued explaining. "The Christmas tree ornaments are small holograms—like the comb I've been wearing in my hair. The holograms make the faces in the ornaments look three-dimensional. And they look like they're moving. My son just started in the business, and he made the ornaments especially for your family."

I turned to Mom and Dad. "But why did Aunt Bergen bring all this stuff to our house?" I asked.

"That's a good question," Mom said.

Aunt Bergen grinned broadly and said, "Conner, you of all people should know why."

"But I don't," I said.

"Remember what you said about Christmas? It's become a holiday about presents. We both agreed the best presents were the ones you gave of yourself," she reminded me.

"I do remember that conversation. That was before I decided you were out to get me," I confessed.

Everyone laughed.

"The meaning of Christmas is giving. At the first Christmas, God gave of himself. He gave us the Christ child, the best gift of all. I brought all my things to your house because my Christmas gift to the Morgan family is myself. I wanted to give you my magic tricks and Boris because they are a part of me." She smiled again.

"The elves you saw running around are some dear friends. They used to be part of my traveling show. They dropped by to help me get my act ready for you and your family."

I stood up and smiled. I was glad to finally know what was going on. My *first* instincts about Aunt

Bergen had been the right ones. I did like her. And I was glad she helped me remember what Christmas was really all about.

I got up to get Aunt Bergen's present to put under the tree. She had propped Boris up in the chair next to it. I looked over at him, smiled, and said, "Have yourself a merry little Christmas, Boris."

As I left the room, a high, strange voice said, "Have yourself a *Merry* little Christmas, Conner."

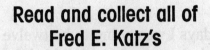

Birthday Cake and I Scream

Book #7

In a few days I was going to be twelve years old. You'd think that a guy's twelfth birthday should be special. I expected mine to be, but the best places to hold a party weren't cooperating.

I wanted to take a huge group of friends to play paintball. But when my mom called Pete's Paintball, it already had a party booked for Friday night.

Mom and I called all over town after that, looking for a fun place to celebrate my birthday. But we kept hearing over and over, "Sorry, but we're booked that night."

I had completely run out of ideas and hated the thought of having a kids' party at home. My folks and I live in a small house with a little yard. It's too small for the number of friends I wanted to include. I'd have to uninvite a bunch of friends. I thought that would be the worst thing in the world. That is until Mom gave me the "good news."

When I came home from school, I tossed my backpack on the floor by the door and headed to the kitchen. After a long day at school and soccer practice, I needed to refuel with chocolate chip cookies and a big glass of milk.

As I poured myself a tall glass of cow juice, Mom came home from work. She didn't even put her brief-case down before she excitedly said, "Kiddo (she always calls me Kiddo, but you can call me Mac—MacKenzie Richard Griffin's the name), I have good news for the birthday boy."

"You decided to get me a four-wheeler?" I jok-ingly asked.

"Even better—I found a place for your party."

My face lit up, and my feet felt like dancing. "Where?"

"Spookie the Clown's Halls of Pizza," she an-nounced with a beaming smile.

My face went gray and my dancing feet became lead. "Mom, we can't go there!" I said.

She knit her brows in puzzlement and asked, "Why?"

"It's for little kids," I protested. "I'll be the laughing-stock of the century."

"Don't worry. You and your friends will have the entire Halls of Pizza to yourselves." Mom smiled. "And Spookie the Clown told me they have a room filled with the latest video games. They even have your favorite, Guardians."

"Guardians? They've got Guardians? Hardly any-one has that one."

Mom made a good argument. If we had the place to ourselves, we wouldn't be bothered by little kids. And the games didn't hurt. But I wasn't convinced. "What about the important stuff like—"

"Like good food?" Mom interrupted. "You'll have all the pizza you can eat. Speaking of which, if we want to eat tonight, I better get moving." Mom grabbed her briefcase and headed to her bedroom to change.

I sat at the kitchen table thinking while I polished off my glass of milk and three cookies. Mom had convinced me that Spookie's place could be fun. Could I convince my friends?

I felt uneasy, so I decided I'd wait until lunchtime the next day to tell anyone. Lots of people had planned to come to my party on Friday night. Would they change their minds when I told them to meet me at a little kids' place?

My morning classes went fast. As much as I liked lunchtime, I hadn't looked forward to this one. I was lost in thought when I heard Frankie call out, "Hey, this way."

I snapped my head up and noticed that I had almost walked right past our table. I gave her and my best friend, Barry, an embarrassed smile.

"Earth to MacKenzie, earth to MacKenzie," Barry said, imitating the scratchy sound of an old science fiction movie. "Please land at your earliest convenience."

I started to absently sit down and nearly plopped down on Lisa. She had slipped into the seat as I was snapping out of my what-do-I-tell-my-friends trance. "Sorry, Lisa. I didn't see you come up behind me."

Lisa smiled at me as I settled into the chair next to hers. I was with my three closest friends, and I dreaded what I had to say.

Barry Lennon had seen most of my twelve years with me. He lived right behind me. We'd played together, gone to the same schools, and attended the same Bible class at church for as long as I could remember.

Frankie and Lisa were cousins. They went to our church too. Lisa spent a lot of time at Frankie's house, which was only a few blocks from my house. Barry and I often walked down to join them. And, since they shared the last name Grey, the girls and I had sat next to each other in all of our elementary school classes. Our teachers had this thing about seating us alphabetically. Frankie and Lisa were the most fun girls I knew.

The four of us played on the same ball teams and attended the same youth group. I guess a person could say that we were inseparable. I hated to tell them my news about Spookie's.

"I have some bad news," I began as a warning. That immediately got everyone's attention. I was ready to drop the news about Spookie's.

Then Davis Wong scooted into the seat at the end of the table and asked, "So, when do I get my paintball gun, and who wants to get hit first?"

Davis was the most recent addition to our group. He had just started at the school this year; his dad was our new vice principal. We met him during the summer at a youth group meeting. He was a pretty cool kid, but he had a crazy sense of humor.

I didn't know what to do. Without stopping to think, I blurted out, "The paintball place is booked."

"What?" Frankie cried out.

"No paintball?" Davis's mouth drooped into a gigantic frown.

"Are you kidding?" Barry asked.

"No, I'm not kidding. We tried everywhere. I guess this was a popular weekend for parties. Everybody had something going on this Friday night," I reported sorrowfully.

"So, what are you going to do?" Frankie asked with genuine concern.

"We got Spookie the Clown's Halls of Pizza," I answered.

Frankie asked, "Isn't that the new place in that old building on Tremble Avenue?"

"That's the one," I responded.

Lisa gasped and got a terribly serious look on her face. Then she sat up straight and said firmly, "No, not Spookie's. Anyplace but Spookie the Clown's Halls of Pizza.

"I figured some people wouldn't want to go because it's a little kids' place," I said. I slumped lower and lower in my chair.

Lisa shot back, "No, that's not it at all. It has nothing to do with little kids. Spookie the Clown's Halls of Pizza is haunted!"

"Come on, Lisa, you don't really believe those silly stories, do you?" Frankie asked.

"I've heard that some pretty strange things have gone on in that old building," her cousin said defensively.

"What happens, do ghosts jump out of pizzas to scare kids?" Davis quipped.

"Don't joke, Davis. There's something very unusual about that building. Nothing stays in business there very long," Barry said.

"Remember, last year? Uncle Andy's House of Sandwiches only lasted about four months. When we were little kids, it was the Chunks of Cheese Pizza Parlor. I can't remember all the names that came in between."

Davis looked puzzled. He asked, "Why do you think so many places go out of business there?"

"It's simple," Lisa stated sharply. "The building is haunted, and the ghosts scare away customers."

In all my planning for my birthday party I hadn't stopped to consider that Spookie's was located in the old Tremble Avenue building.

When my friends and I were a lot younger, the older kids used to tell us stories about that place. They scared us with their talk about ghosts. But that was years ago. We were the older kids now.

Surely Lisa and Barry didn't still believe those crazy stories. Besides, we'd given our lives to Christ. Believing in ghosts and Jesus at the same time just didn't fit.

"Do you think the ghosts are still there? Do you think they'll make a special appearance at Mac's party?" Barry asked us.

The bell rang before anyone could respond to Barry's question. As I walked down the hallway to my next class, I thought about the ghost stories the older kids used to tell us. There were nights when I had to keep a light on in my room because I was so scared. I felt a shiver run up my spine.

Get a grip on reality, Mac, I told myself. *You've given your life to the Lord, and you're too old to be spooked by silly ghost stories.*

The rest of the school day seemed pretty routine. Even soccer practice just sort of slipped by. We covered the same drills over and over. I guess the coach was looking for perfection, but today my heart just wasn't in the game. I was glad to get out of there.

After practice, I hurried to meet Frankie and Lisa at the town library. We had some research to do for a history report. I had chosen them as study partners because they were the two smartest students in the class.

When I got to the library, they had already started on the report. "Sorry, the practice went long," I said after I greeted them. "How's the report coming?"

"Not too bad. We've found a lot of information on the Civil War. Our biggest problem is narrowing things down to a single topic," Lisa said.

"Maybe I can help," I offered.

"We were hoping you might contribute something to this team," Frankie said with a grin. "You could start by digging through these books."

Before I sat down, I said, "I saw another book last week that had some unusual Civil War stories in it. It's up on the third floor. It'll only take me a second to grab it."

I remembered that the book had lots of personal stories in it. Some quotes from people who had fought in the war could make our report outstanding.

Most people avoided the third floor, with its stacks of musty-smelling books. But I liked to prowl and see what new worlds I could discover on the shelves upstairs. I remembered the book was somewhere in the left corner of the building.

The third floor seemed unusually dim today. After

all our talk at lunch about ghosts, the darkness spooked me a little. I walked very slowly between the shelves, listening carefully for sounds that didn't belong in a library.

Finding the book wasn't going to be as easy as I thought. It wasn't where I remembered. I kneeled, trying to focus on the book spines in the dim light.

Suddenly, a large shadow cut off my light. I immediately felt alarmed. *What had made the shadow?* I looked up but couldn't see anything.

I told myself I was being silly. It was probably just someone looking for a book like I was. I went back to my search.

I found the book and reached for it with relief.

Then something blocked the light again. This time, when I looked up, I saw a dark form. It did not look like a person's shadow. It looked like it had wings.

Gripping my book, I stood up and backed against the wall. The thing moved between the rows of bookshelves—toward me. The shadow shivered as it approached. *Had it seen me?*

I scanned the shelves. I wondered if I could climb them and get away. If I tossed books at the approaching menace, would it run?

The form took two more steps and stopped. I placed my foot on one of the shelves to start climbing. But the shelf bowed with my weight. It would never support me. I had to find another escape route.

I grabbed the heaviest books I could find and waited. If the ghoul came any closer, I was going to clobber it. I heard it taking slow, deep breaths. I wondered if it could hear that my heart had begun to beat like a wild conga drum.

The shadowy figure lunged toward me.

I tensed and aimed a heavy book at the shape. Before I could throw it, black cloth fluttered down toward me. In a panic, I fought my way free. In the next second, I realized what had happened.

"That was just a little birthday scare for you," Frankie said through her snorts of laughter.

The girls had threaded long rulers through the arms of Lisa's black raincoat. That's why it looked like it had wings. They had used the spooky shape to scare me.

"Hey, that wasn't funny at all. A guy can get really tense backed into a dark corner like that. If I had hit you with that big book, I could have really hurt you," I chastised them both.

Lisa reached out and took the heavy book from my hands. She looked at the cover, and her eyes grew wide. "Very appropriate, MacKenzie. Did you choose this book on purpose?"

"No, I just grabbed a fat one. What is it?" I asked.

Frankie took the book from Lisa. She turned the spine my way. I read the title: *Our Town's Ghosts and Ghouls: And Their Favorite Haunts.*